The Sand Witch

Alan MacDonald

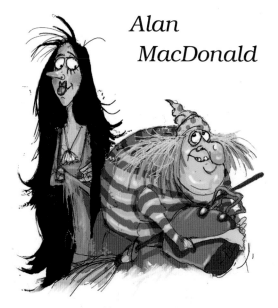

Illustrated by
Chris Mould

OXFORD
UNIVERSITY PRESS

Great Clarendon Street, Oxford, OX2 6DP,
United Kingdom

Oxford University Press is a department of the University of Oxford.
It furthers the University's objective of excellence in research, scholarship,
and education by publishing worldwide. Oxford is a registered trade mark of
Oxford University Press in the UK and in certain other countries

British Library Cataloguing in Publication Data
Data available

978-0-19-276528-4

1 3 5 7 9 10 8 6 4 2

Paper used in the production of this book is a natural, recyclable product
made from wood grown in sustainable forests. The manufacturing process
conforms to the environmental regulations of the country of origin.

Printed in China

Acknowledgements
Cover and inside illustrations by Chris Mould
Background images by Shutterstock
Series editor: Alison Sage

Helping your child to read

Before they start

- Talk about the back cover blurb. What kind of spell might help Drusilla get rid of Hagbag?

- Look at the front cover. Does the woman in the picture look like a witch? Why, or why not?

During reading

- Let your child read at their own pace – don't worry if it's slow. They could read silently, or read to you out loud.
- Help them to work out words they don't know by saying each sound out loud and then blending them to say the word, e.g. *s-w-i-m-s-ui-t, swimsuit.*
- If your child still struggles with a word, just tell them the word and move on.
- Give them lots of praise for good reading!

After reading

- Look at page 32 for some fun activities.

Chapter One

One morning, a letter arrived for
Drusilla. It said:

> THE SAND WITCH
> THE BLACK BEACH HUT
> MUDLEY-ON-SEA

Drusilla opened it up.

"That's odd," she said to her cat, Peg.
"Where's the letter? There's only a crayon
in here."

The crayon jumped out of her hand.
It started writing on the wall.

"Oh, no! Not Hagbag!" groaned
Drusilla. "I hope she doesn't want to stay
for long."

All of a sudden, there was a puff of blue smoke. Hagbag had arrived. She was a large witch with three chins and purple hair.

"Drusilla, you old witch!" cackled Hagbag. She gave Drusilla a hug that nearly squeezed the life out of her.

Hagbag plumped herself down in Drusilla's rocking chair. Peg leaped off with a yowl.

"Scram, cat!" cried Hagbag.

She turned to Drusilla. "Now, what's for breakfast, ducky? I'm starving."

Hagbag sat at the table while Drusilla waited on her. She ate ten slices of toast and a whole jar of jellyfish jam. She drank six mugs of seaweed tea and gobbled all the crab cakes.

At last, Hagbag smacked her lips and said that she was full up.

"Now, ducky," she said. "What do you do for fun around here?"

"I'm afraid you'll be bored," said Drusilla. "It's so quiet by the sea."

"Perfect," said Hagbag. "I need a good rest. I may stay for a week."

Drusilla turned pale. Peg slunk out the door in a sulk. A whole *week*? How could they stand a whole week of Hagbag?

Chapter Two

Hagbag spent the next day lazing on the
beach. She borrowed Drusilla's swimsuit.
Somehow she squeezed herself into it.
She settled into Drusilla's deckchair. Then
she read Drusilla's new Spell Book.

"Well, this *is* a treat," she said. "I'm
going to like it here."

But after five minutes Hagbag
was hungry.

"Do you know what I fancy?" she said.

"A nice ice cream. Be a poppet and get
me one, Drusilla."

Drusilla walked all the way to the shops.
She carried back two dripping ice creams.
One for Hagbag and one for herself.

"Two? You *are* spoiling me!" said
Hagbag. She grabbed both the ice creams.
She started to eat them.

Drusilla and Peg watched her hungrily.
Hagbag didn't even offer them a lick.

All day, Drusilla fetched and carried
things for Hagbag. Every time she sat down,
Hagbag would think of something else.

"Got any sun cream, ducky?" she'd ask.

Or, "Did I hear you say tea?"

By the end of the day, Drusilla was worn
out. It was a relief when Hagbag said she
was ready for bed. She started to climb the
stairs to Drusilla's bedroom.

"Where are you going?" asked Drusilla.

"To bed of course, ducky!"

"But I've only got one hammock …" began Drusilla.

"Don't worry, that'll do me fine. Night night, Drusie. Sleep tight!"

Hagbag got into Drusilla's pyjamas. She climbed into Drusilla's hammock.

Soon, the whole hut shook with the sound of her horrible snoring.

Drusilla put her fingers in her ears.
Peg hid his head under a cushion.
It was no good. There was no chance
of any sleep with Hagbag
in the house.

"That settles it, Peg," said Drusilla.
"We've *got* to get rid of her. The question
is, how?"

Drusilla's Spell Book lay on the table.
Peg leaped on top of it.

He miaowed loudly.

"Of course, you clever cat!" said
Drusilla. "We'll make a spell to drive
Hagbag away."

Drusilla looked through her Spell
Book. Could she turn Hagbag into a large
brown rat? Maybe not. Hagbag might
move in forever and nibble all her food.

Drusilla went on turning the pages.
At last, she found the spell she was
looking for.

"Perfect!" she said. "We'll make her think she's got the Squoozles. I know just how to do it."

All night, Drusilla was mixing something in her big pot and singing her spell.

Chapter Three

Next morning, Hagbag came downstairs.
There was a surprise waiting for her. On
the table was a cake.

It looked like any ordinary cake, except
that it had green spots.

"A cake! For me?" said Hagbag, licking
her lips greedily.

She took a closer look. "Should it be
green?" she asked, doubtfully.

"Oh, yes," said Drusilla. "But I'll eat it myself if you don't want it."

"No, no!" said Hagbag, quickly. "I'll try a little piece."

She cut herself a fat slice and took a bite. "Mmm," she said, with her mouth full. "Not bad."

She cut herself a second slice even bigger than the first. That went into her mouth. So did a third slice and a fourth.

Before long, only a few crumbs were left on the plate. Hagbag had scoffed the whole cake – just as Drusilla knew she would.

In the cake was Drusilla's spell. And now the magic started to do its work.

Hagbag's face turned yellow. Then it went a deep shade of pink.

More and more spots started to appear on her face.

Large, green spots, like those on the cake.

Soon, she was covered in spots.

Hagbag pulled out a tissue. She saw her
hand. "Spots!" she shrieked in horror. "I've
got spots!"

She sat down. "I don't feel too well,
ducky," she said.

Drusilla tried not to smile. She gave
Hagbag a mirror so that she could
see herself.

"I'm afraid you've got the Squoozles,"
said Drusilla.

"The Squoozles? Odds frogs! What's that?"

"Nasty spots," said Drusilla. "Your legs
go wobbly and your knees go knobbly.
I expect you want to go straight home."

"Home?" croaked Hagbag. "But I'll be
all on my own at home!"

"But …" said Drusilla.

"No, no. I'm staying here till I'm better," said Hagbag. "*You* can look after me."

Hagbag crept upstairs.

Drusilla put a hand to her head. What had she done? Her spell had made things much worse. A healthy Hagbag was bad enough. A Hagbag who thought she was ill would be unbearable!

Chapter Four

At first, Hagbag said she was too hot.
Drusilla opened all the windows. Soon,
Hagbag was too cold. She wanted the
windows closed.

Her stomach ached, her toes tingled and
her head throbbed. The sun was too bright.
The hammock was too hard.
The seagulls made too much noise.

One minute she was hungry. The next she wanted a drink.

So it went on all day. Hagbag gave orders and Drusilla dashed up and down the stairs.

At long last, Drusilla heard the sound of snoring. Hagbag had fallen asleep.

Drusilla crept downstairs. She had never felt so tired in her life. She hadn't even had time to eat a meal.

She cleared Hagbag's dirty plates from the table. One of the plates had a few crumbs left on it.

Drusilla hungrily tipped them into her mouth. She sat down in her chair and closed her eyes.

The crumbs in her mouth tasted like cake. Sleepily, she remembered what kind of cake it was. Green spotted cake! The cake that she'd baked for Hagbag.

Chapter Five

In the morning, Hagbag bounded downstairs.

"I'm better, ducky," sang Hagbag. "The spots have gone. I may even stay for two weeks …" She broke off and stared at Drusilla.

Her mouth had dropped open.

"What's the matter?" asked Drusilla.

"The spots! The Squoozles!" gasped Hagbag.

"They're all gone. You're better,"
said Drusilla.

"Not me! *You*, Drusilla! You've caught
the Squoozles!"

Drusilla looked in her mirror. It was
true. Her face was covered in bright green
spots. The crumbs of cake she'd eaten
had been enough to work the spell.

Hagbag backed away from her.

"You poor old thing! What a shame!
I'd love to stay longer but those
Squoozles are obviously catching."
She grabbed her bag.

"Bye, bye, Drusie, I must fly!"
There was a puff of blue smoke.

Hagbag vanished as suddenly as
she'd arrived.

Drusilla went upstairs to her very own bedroom. She climbed into her very own hammock. She didn't mind having spots. They would only last a day.

All that mattered was that Hagbag had gone.

Peg jumped up on to her lap. He started to purr. Drusilla smiled.

It was going to be a quiet day in Mudley-on-Sea.

After reading activities

Quick quiz

See how fast you can answer these questions!
Look back at the story if you can't remember.

 1 Where does Drusilla live?

 2 How does Drusilla feel when Hagbag says she might stay for a week?

 3 Why does Hagbag go home in the end?

Try this!

- Make up a menu of disgusting witchy food for Hagbag.

- You could draw some pictures of the food to decorate the menu!

1) Mudley-on-Sea; 2) worried and fed up; 3) she doesn't want to catch the Squoozles from Drusilla